Samuel C. Hall

Rhymes in Council

aphorisms versified

Samuel C. Hall

Rhymes in Council
aphorisms versified

ISBN/EAN: 9783337264437

Printed in Europe, USA, Canada, Australia, Japan

Cover: Foto ©Andreas Hilbeck / pixelio.de

More available books at **www.hansebooks.com**

Anna Maria Hall

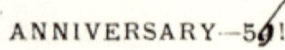

ANNIVERSARY—56!

Yes! we go gently down the hill of life,
  And thank our God at every step we go:
The husband-lover and the sweetheart-wife.
  Of creeping age what do we care or know?
Each says to each, "Our fourscore years.
          thrice told,
Would leave us young: ' the Soul is never old!

What is the Grave to us? can it divide
  The destiny of two by God made one?
We step across, and reach the other side,
  To know our blended life is but begun.
These fading faculties are sent to say
Heaven is more near to-day than yesterday.

S. C. HALL.

S. C. Hall.

Anna Maria Hall.

her autograph S C Hall

S. C. Hall.

To Edward Dinham
with the best wishes
and sincere regards
of his friend
the author
S. C. Hall

RHYMES IN COUNCIL.

Aphorisms Versified.

—

185.

—

"Till old Experience do attain
To something like prophetic strain."
MILTON.

BY

S. C. HALL, F.S.A.

GRIFFITH AND FARRAN,
WEST CORNER OF ST. PAUL'S CHURCHYARD, LONDON.
E. P. DUTTON & CO., NEW YORK.
1881.

CHISWICK PRESS :— C. WHITTINGHAM AND CO., TOOKS COURT,
CHANCERY LANE, LONDON.

THIS BOOK OF

VERSIFIED APHORISMS

IS, BY DIRECT SANCTION

OF HER MAJESTY,

Dedicated

TO THE GRANDCHILDREN OF

THE QUEEN.

In the eighty-first year of my age, I write these VERSES; they are the out-come of knowledge, based on experience, and matured by thought : the proceeds of A LONG LIFE.

A few dotted down reflections have grown into a Book.

I bequeath them as a LEGACY to my kind—with humility, but with faith, hope, trust, and love.

May they, by the aid and blessing of God, bear fruit!

Since they were written,—while they were passing through the press,—the partner of my pilgrimage, the participator in all my labours and cares, my companion, friend, counsellor, and wife, during fifty-six years, has been removed from earth and from me, from many friends who dearly loved her, and from a public by whom she was largely appreciated since the publication of her first Book (—followed by, I think, two hundred and fifty Books—) in the far-off year 1828. These verses are hardly less hers than mine. If I have striven— in humble, but fervent and prayerful, hope—to inculcate rectitude, goodness, love, sympathy, gentle and generous thinking, humanity, patience, virtue, and piety, Faith, Hope, and Charity—my work was suggested, encouraged, sustained—I will reverently add, inspired—by her.

This Book, therefore, although written by me, I hope may be regarded as a MONUMENT TO HER MEMORY.

APHORISMS VERSIFIED:

CONCERNING

RHYMES IN COUNCIL.

I.

THIS is the Golden Rule: "To others do
As you would have the others do to you."
But old Experience, Wisdom, Love, and Truth,
Give added Rules to guide and govern Youth.

II.

Abundant themes press on me. I bequeath
An old man's Legacy—of pen and tongue:
In loving words, yet forceful: hope to breathe
Into their ears and hearts—and teach the Young.
Sermons the words may be—though preached in rhyme:
The fruitage of Experience, brought by Time.
Wise rules and maxims, garbed in humble dress.
God guide me—as I labour—to express
Only the thought and counsel He will bless!

III.

Two sterling truths, impressed in simple rhymes—
Two fertile truths—may well my task begin:
Neglected opportunities are crimes,
Omitted duty is committed sin.

B

IV.

None are so base or low they nothing teach :
A sun-glimpse may the loftiest glacier reach.
Let " Hope " be on all banners—when unfurled !
A POOR UNLETTERED TINKER TAUGHT A WORLD !

V.

TROUBLES are often BLESSINGS in disguise :
    To Souls a healthful discipline they bring :
May come, as rain-showers come, from sun-lit skies,
    Or fall, as balm-drops, from an Angel's wing.
Though Wisdom fail to track the ways of God,
Mercy can send the staff—that seems a rod !
Adversity may keep, yet hide, its light :
Stars always shine, though only seen at night.

VI.

ADVERSITY the worth of metal tries :
Base metal better metals purifies.
We do not dread the sea when waves are calm :
    Nor forest shelter seek when winds are hushed :
    Flowers send their sweetest odours out when crushed :
The wounded tree supplies the healing balm.

VII.

Troubles that sadden and perplex to-day,
Wait till to-morrow, may have passed away.
And happiness—the present moment's joy—
Be but prophetic warning of alloy.
Hope will supply the Amaranthine wreath ;
And Faith the sword of Damocles may sheath.

VIII.

In the right path walk firmly, without fear:
EXCELSIOR may be written PERSEVERE.
All good resolves will strengthen while they keep:
Like planted trees they grow while planters sleep.
FORCED KNOWLEDGE may be first steps to a tomb:
There's no endurance in a hot-house bloom.

IX.

Study DOMESTIC DUTIES: it is wise,
As well as prudent, to economize:
For " what you save you have," and so may share
That which Extravagance can seldom spare.

X.

Yet PRUDENCE need not be unwholesome thrift:
To save may not be mean: the best will see
The rainy day that comes to man and bee:
But God and man abhor a burthened gift.
And those who test the truth, the truth believe—
" More blessed 'tis to give than to receive ! "

XI.

All good work must result from LABOUR: none
Can see a good work in a moment done:
Mere trifles cost the nothing they are worth:
The lion gives but one cub at a birth:
Eagles, 'tis said, lay three eggs, and hatch one.

XII.

Brief but despotic is the SLUGGARD's reign:
   Nature is never idle: worse than crime
   Is IDLENESS—a waste of God-given time:
A rot of mind, a mildew of the brain.
With drowsy lounge, his laggard limbs he drags:
The IDLER pays a large price for his rags.

XIII.

Some men exhaust in SLOTH their natural powers:
   To some a day is wearisome by length:
   While some from ardent labour gather strength.
Men may be young in years, yet old in hours:
Youth may with well-earned laurel-wreaths be graced,
And Age be nothing but protracted waste.

XIV.

HARD WORK is healthful; never kills: but SLOTH
Is fatal to the mind and body—both:
   Mix labour, ease, and pleasure; wise men say,
   Eight hours to each—to sleep, to work, to play—
   Make the sum total of a well-spent day.

XV.

Work! Self-help is the Law that governs man;
The base and ground-work of God's perfect plan:
His will is that we work for what we ask;
Work with our hands or heads: nor shirk the task.
   Work! Work! that with a boon a blessing brings:
   Work is the lot of all created things—
   The earliest mandate of the King of Kings!

XVI.

From seed not planted, will you look for flowers?
No God-help without self-help can be ours.
   Think how you best may plant the pregnant seed:
   And God will give the strength the weak ones need:
   A Titan can move nothing with a reed.

XVII.

A wretched faith is their faith who believe
The Vineyard workers small rewards receive;
That God neglects the servants He engages
To do His work—and grudges them their wages!

XVIII.

When Death removes the Soul from homes of clay,
   And we in spirit-homes our lives renew,
When earth's dark hours are changed to perfect day,
   Be sure our God will give us work to do:
Continued work—of mind, heart, tongue, or pen.
We may be teaching still our fellow men—

And fellow men the words of truth may read,
Where He who lights the lamp, the flame will feed.
No life apart from labour can be blest:
Nor USELESS IDLENESS be HAPPY REST.

XIX.

Faith, Hope, and Charity will blessings be ;
But CHARITY is greatest of " the Three !"
Ah! not the Charity that gives with frowns,
    And wears a garb the Heaven-descended scorns ;
Ah! not the fœtid Charity that crowns
    The Lord—Almighty LOVE Himself—with thorns :
Impedes the victor as he nears the goal,
And lends a broken anchor to the Soul :
It is the hallowed Charity that gives
A sympathetic help TO ALL THAT LIVES.

XX.

Those who the naked clothe, the hungry feed,
Will they by PROXY help, when sufferers need,
And do their work by deputy—content
To see their doles by some " Committee " spent ;
Relieve by " rule," well " organized," and planned,
And buy a batch of blessings—second hand ?

XXI.

BENEVOLENCE ! BENEFICENCE ! to few
There seems distinction : but one feels : one gives :
The one is transient, but the other lives.

One may relieve, and nothing give : the other
May give, and not relieve, a needing brother :
Though oft, thank God, the two will work together.
One may be storm-shower, and the other dew :
  One may be honey, and the other gall :
The large gifts of the rich were gifts but small :
  The widow's offering was the widow's all.

XXII.

" Blest be the merciful ! " who do
  God's earth work ; practise what they preach ;
Giving to many—as to few—
  The Universal LOVE they teach.
Not men alone are they who think
  Good " Neighbours " bid STREET FOUNTAINS flow ;
They thank the taught of God, who drink,
  And, grateful, to their labour go.
Women and children, babes at breast,
  In words, or lisps, record a joy !
With thanks—instinctively expressed—
  By thoughtless girl, and reckless boy.
Horses, o'erladen, weary, worn,
  Drink nectar-draughts : and go their way :
Refreshed at noon-day, night and morn ;
  Need we translate the grateful neigh ?
And the good dog—true friend of man—
  Laps : thanks ! Laps ! thanks, again ! and—hark !
He gives the giver all he can,
  A gleeful and a grateful bark !

Birds dip their beaks; their heads they raise:
   And chirp a blessing: flap the wing:
Then flutter with thanksgiving-praise:
   And, though but pariahs, try to sing.
While cattle, goaded through the street,
   Way-worn with thirst—foretasting death:
Grateful, the fountain-givers greet:
   It may be with a latest breath.
All nature joins to bless the thought
   That gave the blessing—blest of God!
When Wisdom, led by Mercy, brought
   A " staff," sustaining—not a rod.
God bless the Donors! one and all!
   Who give the water—freely quaffed;
To creatures large, and creatures small,
   They bring the pure, refreshing draught!

God bless the Donors! one and all!

XXIII.

MANNER will often gain more friends than MATTER;
To make men self-pleased need not be to flatter:
For FLATTERY is filth that must degrade
The giver and the taker; 'tis the trade
Of grovelling souls that cannot walk upright.
   But *wish to please* may grace the worthiest man,
   May be of Life the healthiest, best, ground-plan;
It gives the structure substance, air, and light!

XXIV.

SINCERITY that would CONVICTION bring,
Must be a gentle and a generous thing :
Reproof as far from rudeness as from guile :
Surgeons who probe a death-wound will not smile.
True, kindly, COURTESY no rank can soil :
For Nature's gentlemen may live by toil :
POLITENESS nothing costs, yet buys a deal,
Though but an echo of what good men feel.

XXV.

MEEKNESS may be Dictator—unaware !
Ten men are led where one is driven :—beware
  Of asking aid from force, where you would lead :
  Harsh measures often fail where smooth succeed.
  The gentle dew will fructify the seed,
  While heavy showers oppress the plants they feed.

XXVI.

GIFTS may be burthened, and so lose their charm ;
And where they would do service may do harm :
  May not be measured out with grudging thrift :
The manner is ungracious, that is all :
And so the honey may be mixed with gall :
No boons as burthens should recipients feel :
  A diamond carcanet may be a gift
Less precious than a simple link of steel.

XXVII.

SMALL THINGS may best sustain and sweeten life,
However small, they bar the way to strife :
They are what streams are to the rapid rivers :
 They flow to fertilize a thousand places
 The river cannot reach : where the eye traces
 The verdure nourished in the cheerful meads,
 Green meadows, every tiny streamlet feeds,
And banks and braes that bless the bounteous givers.

XXVIII.

 Not for ourselves alone we live :
 The Master gives that we may give :
 To think, and feel, for all who need :
 Help-giving, not in word but deed.
 " Faith without works is dead," we know :
 And we, by works, our Faith must show :
 In making happy, Heaven begins :
 GOD-LOVE and NEIGHBOUR-LOVE are twins.
 Can we see Want and Pain and Grief,
 And safe in self, bring no relief?
 Can we ask blessings of our God,
 His staff for us, for them His rod?
 Shall we, who take the boons divine,
 Be numbered with the thankless nine?
 Content to walk in pleasant ways,
 With formal words of barren praise?
 The cruse of oil will not be less
 That feeds a brother in distress :

Nor will the generous mind and heart
Be poorer that they share a part.
The gifts we give to those who need
Will be, to us, the fruit of seed :
Fourfold the recompense will be,
For what we give we LEND TO THEE !

XXIX.

Some men demand rough treatment—everywhere :
   Will apples tempt a wild boar to a stye ?
You cannot with a whistle tame a bear:
   You cannot with a beckon lure a fly :
You cannot with a straw-plait bind a man :
You do not brain a mad dog with a fan.
Yet gentleness may work where force will fail ;
And kindness, patience, " suffering-long," prevail.

XXX.

But gentle LENIENCY TO VICE is crime :
   A crime that mutiny of soul has reared,
A crime that grows nor less nor weak with time,
   A crime that Truth entangles, Virtue wrongs:
You will not seize a lion by the beard,
   Nor grasp a cobra with a sugar tongs.

XXXI.

Take this to heart!—that LOYALTY is now
   The easiest of our duties ; every home
   Finding its model in the stateliest dome :

While life's more humble cares exampled are
By one who rules o'er millions—near and far.
But look not back : it was not always so :
Look forward : from good roots good branches grow.
First thank your God who blessed this happy land ;
   Next that your brave forefathers made you free ;
Next for a Constitution, wisely planned,—
   Queen, Lords, and Commons, that make ONE OF THREE !

XXXII.

Those who are British-born and British-bred,
May cherish holy pride ; they do not dread
A despot in a Crowned Republic ; they
Only the laws, themselves have made, obey ;
For freedom is their birth-boon ; to do right,
And wrong eschew, is safeguard—sound and sure—
That guards the rich no better than the poor.

XXXIII.

PRIDE is to Vanity as gold to brass,
Or as the ripened corn to withered grass :
The proper pride, that can do nothing mean ;
   As far removed from meanness as from shame :
A pride that but with loftier minds is seen,
   That seeks no praise, but earns unconscious fame ;
Never self-confident, though self-confiding,
By honour guided, and to honour guiding.

XXXIV.

But VANITY's a sneak, a thing of straw,
  Padded with chaff; stuff'd out to look the real:
The peacock's feathers, mounted on a daw;
  Of insignificance, the " beau-ideal."
Perpetual checks, continual puttings down,
Make Vanity a curse, from peer to clown.

XXXV.

Let PRIDE not be the pride that looks with scorn
On men more humbly bred or lowly born;
That courts, with sneering smiles and knitted brow,
And says, give place to " holier men than thou."
Let *your* pride be the pride that shrinks from wrong,
That woos nor single culprit nor a throng;
The pride that grandly, *proudly*, walks aside
And seeks associate worthies—that is PRIDE!

XXXVI.

Your SELF-ESTEEM in due subjection hold:
  Learn when you may advance, and when retire:
And where your betters are, wait to be told,
  In the good Master's words, "Friend, go up higher!"

XXXVII.

Even in SUCCESS be heedful how you boast;
  And in your triumphs be not over-proud:
The stateliest palm-trees feel the tempest most;
  The laurel draws the lightning from the cloud.

XXXVIII.

Let him that standeth take heed lest he fall:
None at day dawn his own the day may call:
And let not him who dons his armour, scoff,
At him who puts his well-worn armour off.
To say " I'm certain," is the right of none.
" I will do" widely differs from " I've done !"

XXXIX.

Much guilt is his who wastes the wealth-source, Time ;
And vague PROCRASTINATION is a crime.
What may be done—and rightly done—to-day,
Postpone not till the morrow: who can say
He will that morrow see, that work to do?
Fore-knowledge is for none : fore-thought for few.

XL.

TIME LOST is LOST for ever : to regain
Time lost—the effort *must* be made in vain.
  As easy 'twere to twist a rope of sand,
  Or gather moisture in a sun-parched land,
Or ice flakes from the genial summer rain.
Time lost—not even Prayer brings back again.

XLI.

" Too LATE !" What solemn truths these two words tell !
Too late is written on the gates of Hell !
Too late is breathed in Heaven by grieving saints !
Too late, when Reason fails and Nature faints !

Too late, when stern Resolve would govern Fate!
  Said in a thousand ways to warn and scare,
  Linked with another awful word—Beware!
Yet all Creation bears the ban—TOO LATE!

XLII.

And do not live to eat; but EAT TO LIVE:
Seek food that natural appetite will give.
The glutton's a low animal, at least,
Who, fed on filthy garbage, makes a feast:
The epicure is happy, now and then,
But wretched in nine cases out of ten.

XLIII.

And let your daily prayer for daily bread
  Be thus accompanied—" May God relieve
The wants of others; " and, when that is said,
  With thanks to God for what yourselves receive,
Say, will your natural appetite be less?
Or food unwholesome you ask God to bless?

XLIV.

Give not to others what you will not touch:
  Even of the wholesome viands shun excess:
  Rich boons are evils if their weight oppress:
More than enough must always be too much.

XLV.

The man who has no foes has earned no friends;
  Has not his duty done—to bad or good:
He must have truckled for his private ends;
  And not the good upheld, the bad withstood.
The man who fears to make a foe, when right
  Commands the risk, is only half a man:
A thing—contemptible to soul and sight;
  A blot to mar God's highest, holiest, plan.
The man who has no enemy must show
  A coward heart, that skulks in Honour's fight;
He who for Justice fails to strike a blow,
Is of all good and upright men the foe.

XLVI.

How oft by one irrevocable word
  The utterer would give millions to recall,
All evil passions of the soul are stirred
  To deaden, or excite to fury—all!
A single word that Angels grieve to hear!
A word that brings Hell's prompters very near!

XLVII.

We may be " angry without sin " we know:
When righteous indignation cause may show:
  When patience from oppression suffers long:
  When justice, outraged, would redress a wrong,
  When the weak ask protection of the strong.

XLVIII.

Ye who would gain inheritance of Heaven,
Hear the Lord's answer to the listening throng!
" How oft shall I forgive my brother's wrong?
Till seven times?   Must my patience last so long?"
  " NOT SEVEN ; BUT SEVENTY, MULTIPLIED BY SEVEN !"
These are His warning words to all who live!
" Forgive and be forgiven !"   That prayer we pray:
Sinners, whose sins augment from day to day ;
Who hear His call yet walk not in His way:
  Shall we ask God for what we do not give?
  The Lesson and Example—both are Thine !
Those who forgive will God-forgiven be.
Lord! teach us to forgive: to learn of Thee !
How very little to forgive have we :
  How much hast Thou to pardon, Lord Divine !

XLIX.

DECISION is what sunlight is to spring ,
But INDECISION is the coward's king :
Infirm of purpose—vacancy of thought—
Hatcher of addled eggs—that bring forth nought.
Yet SELF-EXAMINATION'S always wise,
If but a wholesome mental exercise.

L.

TRUTH will be cheaply bought at any price ;
Be worth its cost at any sacrifice.

Truth, holy truth, abominates disguise;
PREVARICATIONS are the scum of lies.

LI.

TRUTH means the whole truth; nothing but the truth:
The safest and the surest guide to youth;
  'Tis the foundation of all Virtues—all!
Where truth is never—or is seldom—found,
You build the house, but build on sandy ground:
  When the first tempest comes the house will fall!

LII.

Slander! it is a mean, and filthy vice,
That only brutal natures can entice:
That God's law and Man's law alike defies:
To "bear false witness" is the lie of lies.

LIII.

An evil WRITER Satan's labour spares:
  For every printed word becomes a seed
  That, planted, *must* spring up—a flower or weed:
The Devil does not ask "Whence hath it tares?"

LIV.

TALENTS, if unemployed, are curses: none
  Are meant for idle waste, but for employ,
  The Giver means the given to enjoy.

The Lord condemned the man who had received,
But had not used, his talent : who believed
That in returning it enough was done.

LV.

Read much and well digest the books you read :
Such as are fertile yielders of good seed :
But some inculcate error, some mislead,
And some are dæmon work, in thought and deed.
If there be writers—fiend-possessed—who give
A daily curse for every day they live,
Many are they—pure women and good men—
Who combat chiefs of Satan—with the pen !

LVI.

Humanity is love, as God gives love :
    Love to the creatures who can nothing pay ;
    Not even by words a thankful Soul would say :
The debt has record in the Courts above,
And will be paid, in coin that cannot rust :
Paid at the resurrection of the Just.

LVII.

Those who have joy in suffering—seen or heard—
Are blurs on Nature : *see* the stricken bird
Flutter in agony a shattered wing :
Hear him his mournful requiem try to sing !

While knights and dames enjoy the " sport " and cheer
The shot : nor ask " What Dæmon brings us here ? "
Not men and women only: one would think
Devils from such infernal " pleasures " shrink !

LVIII.

Shut not a door to sinners who REPENT ;
The Lord " unto the righteous " was not sent :
A blessed change may come to one and all ;
Remember, Saul of Tarsus was Saint Paul.
" Peace at the last " the peace of God may bring ;
And o'er the soul rejoicing Angels sing.

LIX.

SINNERS to-day, to-morrow may be saints :
Who touched, to heal, the men with leper-taints ?
There may for them be joy in Heaven: for those
You rescue, ere the book of life can close :
And you may hear the triumph-song for him,
A sinner, welcomed by the Seraphim.

LX.

The humblest man may hear the Master say
    Come, " good and faithful servant: enter thou ! "
He answers utter outcasts—when they pray,
    And sinful sisters when the knee they bow :
The very lowest of a trusting throng
To Heaven's blest Hierarchy may yet belong.

LXI.

'Tis true, good words, good thoughts, good counsel, may
Seem on the coarse and sensual thrown away:
    As boons such natures neither ask nor need:
    It may appear as rational to feed
    An ass with venison, or a dog with wine,
    Or fill with orient pearls a trough for swine:
Yet saints to-day were fiends but yesterday!

LXII.

A mutual CONTRACT is a closed affair,
No afterthought may cancel or impair;
For promises are debts, and always were:
    A pledged word is a solemn act and deed;
    A bond the lowest ignorance may read.
Who claims and takes more than his honest share,
Betrays and thieves—yet calls the dealing FAIR!

LXIII.

A bargainer, one-sided, is a knave,
Who means to make a victim or a slave:
Dividing one by two: one large, one small:
He takes his own share, and the lion's—all.
But HONESTY and POLICY are brothers,
The truly just to selves are just to others.

LXIV.

Think not because you keep within the Law
The vessel of your Conscience has no flaw

They are not synonyms—right is not might!
Nor is it always Justice, Law makes right.
Things, many things, there are Law never reaches,
Things vital—God-directed Conscience teaches.

LXV.

CONSCIENCE—a good sub-guide—*may* lead us right ;
But is at best a glowworm in the night,
And rarely shows to us a guiding light ;
But glow-worms, useless as a beacon, may
Supply life-saving light in danger's way.
To silence conscience Nature vainly tries.
Conscience may sleep—but Conscience never dies.

LXVI.

Stern PUNCTUALITY is truth and right :
A virtue—though but little, at first sight.
Its rank among the Virtues may be small,
Yet 'tis a condiment that sweetens all,
Who makes another wait, commits offence
Against good breeding, manners, duty, sense.
A breach of it is falsehood ; moral dearth :
Wicked or weak : no man a doit is worth
Whose bond is any better than his word :
'Tis sacred as if all the world had heard.

LXVII.

Less evil to our "neighbour" may be wrought
By wrong deliberate than by WANT OF THOUGHT :

A Sunday smile may be a Sabbath frown
By the neglected payment of a crown:
  By needless, cruel, often sad, delay,
  Good men have shuddered as they heard men say,
  " Let the man bring his bill another day."

LXVIII.

" Who borrows, sorrows," saith the quaint old rhyme:
And debts there are that touch the barrier—crime:
But there are debts that honour him who lends:
Debts that are never foes—but fertile friends.

LXIX.

His is a miserable soul who tries
  How little he may give for what he gets.
To GIFTS the truth more specially applies:
  All obligations are but honest debts,
Debts which the upright debtor gladly meets.
Those who will try to shirk them are but cheats.

  Pay! pay in kind, if in no coin you pay.:
  Remember they bear interest, day by day!
  Where there's a will, there always is a way.

LXX.

Some men there are who live with hearts of stone,
That neither thrill nor throb: for self alone:
The selfish man is his own curse; and brings
A poison home! distilled from noxious things:

For Nature ever works to blight and ban,
The self-indulgence of the SELFISH MAN.
You will not look for leaves, or flowers, or fruit,
From trees you know are cankered at the root.

LXXI.

'Tis a poor, paltry, guilt to reason thus—
The plagues that plague our neighbours harm not us
Yet callous souls there are who, heedless, see
A far-off famine desolate a land:
A distant earthquake—which they need not fear:
A realm upbroken by a reckless hand:
A ruthless war—of which they only hear:
And feel no more—while they are safe and free—
Than if a passing tempest bared a tree.

LXXII.

To COVET is of thefts the basest kind:
No law can punish where no law can bind:
A coward crime: a cancer of the mind.

LXXIII.

And blear-eyed ENVY is a curse, at best!
If non-infectious, still a moral pest:
A social itch that lets no body rest.

LXXIV.

Rarely is RETROSPECT without a cloud:
  A back look may bring sadness—far or near;

Gloomy reminders, dim amidst a crowd ;
   A still small voice the dark world does not hear.
Control the future thought by good deeds done :
Ponder o'er those you seek, and those you shun.
Conscience may whisper truth—but never loud.
Set free the fount to issue draughts of joy :
Reflection can Despondency destroy.

LXXV.

WEALTH is a blessing, if 'tis rightly used :
A curse unmitigated, if abused.
'Tis simple truth—the richest man is poor
Who needs, or fancies he has need of, more :
   Yearning for that which soul-diseases brings.
All boons are weary heart-sores, when they cloy,
And the pure sources of delight destroy ;
   Perpetual cravings for a thousand things—
Things that the poor man can, and does, enjoy.

LXXVI.

For WEALTH-LOVE of " all evil " is the " root."
   WEALTH-HOARDED, is a blighted tree, that gives
No joy to sight or mind ; nor flower nor fruit ;
   It brings a blessing to no soul that lives.
God sends it to the worthless—(but to show
   How poor the gift—of all His gifts the least).
Thirsty, with muzzled mouths, where fountains flow !
   Hungry, with fettered hands, while near a feast !

LXXVII.

Pity the man who, having much, asks more ;
   Who gets the more, and yet the more will need ;
Whose plethora of riches keeps him poor ;
   Whose craving appetite is boundless greed.
Perpetual want is but continual woe :
Fountains are evils when they overflow.
From poor and rich alike God calls the soul,
And leaves to Earth—not portions, but the whole :
The craftsman's meal-tub and the merchant's store.

LXXVIII.

" He died worth half a million !" and went hence.
With capital sufficient, to commence
A good trade in the world to which he'sped,
Admired, and envied, by the pauper dead !
To die just then *was* hard ; when money lent
Might bring the wary lender cent. per cent.
He tried to bribe grim Death with half his gain,
And offered sundry substitutes : in vain.

LXXIX.

Thrice blessed be the son of Sirac's prayer :
   " Nor poverty, nor riches, Lord ! be mine."
For Dives' light is Hell's pernicious glare :
But Virtue makes the poorest child God's heir

LXXX.

This was the prayer of one I knew : and thus
The prayer was answered—teaching all of us.

"God give me wealth!" in ignorance he prayed:
"Lord! let this plague of poverty be stayed!"
God sent his Angel-messenger, who said,
"Take wealth: I take some other gift instead.
What wilt thou give me in exchange for wealth?
I give thee riches, and take from thee health."
"Not that, O Lord! with that I cannot part:
Health strengthens mind and soul and nerve and heart."
"Then, in exchange, I take thy honoured name,
And leave to thee a heritage of shame."
"My God, have mercy on me! do not so:
Life would be life o'er-burthened, dark and low."
    "So be it: but the friends you love shall go:
I will take them, and leave you all alone."
"No, no! for life would be perpetual moan."
"What wilt thou give me, then, who ask for wealth?
Which of your blessings shall I take?" "Lord, None!
Let me retain my friends, good name, and health:
And keep me poor as now—till life is done."

LXXXI.

Use not the word "IMPOSSIBLE." Who knows?
The things impossible that morning shows
(Because forsooth no "natural" laws obey)
May be a common fact before mid-day!
Impossible! to rush ten thousand miles
And back within the hour: a moderate pace.
Impossible! to paint a human face
In less than half a second—full of smiles.

Impossible ! against the wind and tide
To sail a ship: the main and top masts bare.
Impossible ! to light a town with air
Squeezed from a coal mine, where the coal may bide!

LXXXII.

No doubt, 'twould be agreeable—our knowing
  Things many, great and small, we do not know.
Why gradual growth is part of Nature's plan,
And wasted years must make a babe a man.
Why should not hands and feet continue growing,
  As well as nails and hair, that always grow !
And men be sixty, and not six feet high?
And forest topmost-branches touch the sky?
So, when God speaks in miracles, in vain,
The thoughtless and the foolish say, "Speak plain !"
Ask of ten million things the reason—*why ?*
And take the only answer—IT IS so !

LXXXIII.

Some ruthless hands will take the scythe from Time,
And do his work: nor think such work is crime.

LXXXIV.

Choose your COMPANIONS carefully: for they
  Will tell us what you are or soon will be—
  They make you slaves to habits—bond or free—
As artist hands will mould the potter's clay.

LXXXV.

Remember that EXAMPLES good, are teachers,
More forceful than a thousand able preachers.
That humble virtue may have shown and said
More than the loftiest born and daintiest bred.

LXXXVI.

" HABIT is second Nature !"   Well we know
How vast its power to govern all below.
How hard to bend or break it : well or ill :
It sways us from the cradle to the grave.
We try to rule it, but it rules us still :
Study to be its master, not its slave.

LXXXVII.

But HABITS may be subject to control :
    We guide the greater, and direct the less :
    The good to nurture, and the bad suppress :
The Virtues are but habits of the Soul.

LXXXVIII.

DRESS as becomes your station—high or low :
From dress neglected, sloven habits grow :
Yet little is the gain, while much is lost,
To grace, and art, and taste, by needless cost.

LXXXIX.

No Virtue lives where dangers none exist :
No force of character where none resist.

Firmly and steadily, o'er rocks to tread,
Will make a firm and steady heart and head:
But those who only walk among sweet flowers,
Degenerate, and lose their natural powers.
Storms clear the atmosphere : to breast a storm
Strengthens the limbs, invigorates the form :
While difficulties, meaner minds shrink from,
Are trials sent to meet—and overcome.

XC.

All sinners say they will no farther go
Than so far; where to stop they do not know:
They flatter self, who think the soul can send
    For aid to Penitence—for heart and mind,
    Repent when leisure suits—and when inclined !
Sin is but the beginning of the end.

XCI.

Poor spirits, weak and mean—as mean as weak,
Who know not Justice—are the men who seek
Their God—but only when they want Him : they
Put off acquaintance with Him; day by day :
And yet expect Him to hear all they say !

XCII.

Who ASKS to do a WRONG thing is a foe :
At any cost, the answer must be " No !"

XCIII.

FRIENDSHIP is not like Jonah's gourd, that grew
    And withered in a night: no sudden birth
    May bring assurance of desert and worth.
    On Virtue based it gathers force on Earth;
The strength that Time will test and Heaven renew.
Friends are not quickly made—though quickly lost:
Friends are well worth the largest price they cost.

XCIV.

What a man soweth, that the man shall reap,
    Is the great law of Nature—strong and sound:
Through every change that Law its force will keep.
    Sow only good seed; sow it on good ground;
    And, after time, the harvest *must* be found!

XCV.

Avoid the SCEPTIC; poisoner of the soul;
    A life-curse; taking from us faith and trust
    To prove that dust is animated dust,
    And that HEREAFTER gives no place of rest.
    A social, physical, and moral pest:
A thief of hope in death: a monster ghoul.

XCVI.

But WOMEN-SCEPTICS are fair Nature's blots:
Stars—but of which you only see the spots:
Or trees, that, foully cankered at the root,
Bear only withered leaves and deadly fruit:

Or streams, polluted at their primal source,
That run—a stream of poison—all their course ;
Social mistakes : a dull domestic dearth :
Women who have no Altar, have no Hearth !

XCVII.

For those who have no HOME LOVE, have no love
For aught of Earth below, or Heaven above !
No ties of parent, children, husband, wife,
That bind through life—and through the after-life.
HOME LOVE will take a blessing every where,
To the dark alley or the lordly square.

XCVIII.

Dead trees alone no leaves to Spring give birth :
    No Home need be without its boon of leaven :
Angels who watch the Altar guard the Hearth :
    From a pure Home 'tis but a step to Heaven.

XCIX.

If hallowèd be the Sabbath—let it be
    To love-work dedicate, and holy thought :
    For rest from labour, the sweet day has brought :
The All-Wise gave that blessed boon to thee.
    But those who send Home-cheerfulness away,
    And think hearts are not pure when hearts are gay,
    Insult the LOVE that blessed that HAPPY DAY.

C.

God means us to be happy: God is Love!
Love of all things, around, beneath, above :
God means us to be CHEERFUL ; hopeless gloom
Is the perpetual shadow of a tomb.
God does not tolerate unreasoning sadness :
The lamp of life is fed with oil of gladness.
Those who, self-mortified, His love deny,
Give the All-loving source of Love, the lie.
All nature lives to love : the law He gave,
  "Love one another," rules in every sphere :
Lives through all life ; but ends not with the grave :
  His words the "perfect just" and Angels hear!

CI.

You will not blame the burst of natural GRIEF,
That brings the overburdened Soul relief :
Sorrow is Nature's law—that must have sway :
  The bond of all who live—that must be kept.
Even the Divine to human grief gave way :
  Beside the grave of Lazarus, "Jesus wept."
Grief that resists Religion, Reason, Time,
Is sinful grief that charges God with crime.

CII.

A childless widow, seemingly forsaken,
  Gave words to wrath—rebellious, fierce, and wild :
Wrath that the gift The Giver gave was taken :
  And would not pardon God who took her child.

D

She had a waking-vision: saw a band
   Of happy children: there she knew her boy:
Each held a lighted lamp in his young hand:
   And, as they passed, each sang a hymn of joy.
All but one mournful child: *his* solemn tread,
   And face, were gloom: *his* lamp—it had no light:
When, sobbing through her tears, the mother said,
   " How comes it, dear, your lamp is dark as night?"
" Mother!" he said, "you, mother, make me sad,
   Your tears put out my lamp: and stay my voice:
I must be mournful when I would be glad,
   In silent sorrow, where I should rejoice."
Up rose the mother from her knees, and smiled;
   Her sobs were stilled: of tears remainèd none:
As bending low her head towards her child,
   She clasped her hands and said, HIS WILL BE DONE."
Out burst the lamp, with a wide-spreading light!
   Out burst, from all that group, a joyful hymn!
It changed to perfect day her dismal night,
   When heard and echoed by the Seraphim!

CIII.

" Oh! blessed be my baby boy!"
   Thus spake a mother to her child.
Then kissed him with excess of joy,
   Then looked into his face and smiled.
But as the mother breathed his name—
   The fervent prayer was scarcely said—

Convulsions shook the fragile frame,
The mother's only babe was dead.
Yet still her faith in Him she kept—
In Him who turned to grief her joy;
And still she murmured as she wept,
"Oh! blessed *is* my baby boy."

CIV.

Fear God! but fear not with a dastard fear :
The God all merciful is God all just :
Fear may be love : be linked with faith and trust :
We know, in all our trials, God is near :
We know it—if we *feel* the words He said :
When the storm raged, and hope from man had fled,
The terror-stricken heard Him—"I am here!"

CV.

Few truths than this are wiser or more true :—
'Tis well to have a little more to do
Than you can do conveniently : for trust
In leisure often brings degrading rust.
"Better wear out than rust out!" 'tis a truth
Age should be mindful to impress on youth.

CVI.

Do what you do as well as you can do it.
Call nothing well done that you can do better :
Whether to draw a deed or write a letter.
Your work—go wisely, but go bravely, through it ;

Take as your golden rule, " I do my best !"
Then, to God's guidance you may leave the rest.

CVII.

ZEAL may be over hot; but lukewarm fools
    Have shrivelled hearts, flat heads, and dwindled minds.
One class are rivers, one are stagnant pools,
    One are the juice of good fruit : one its rinds.
You strive to rouse the one—and strive in vain :
The other—Nature-helped—you can restrain,
He needs no spur who heeds the slackened rein.

CVIII.

To all mankind do all the good you can ;
    With joy the staff supply, with grief the rod.
The love of God infers the love of man :
    The love of man infers the love of God.
No man loves God—yet hates or scorns his brother.
GOD-LOVE and BROTHER-LOVE !   One is the other !

CIX.

Give to your SERVANTS needful calm and rest ;
With kind words ever : you will have the best.
Enjoy no comfort where they have no part ;
Give them their wages, but with all your heart.
A bond that merely gives—and takes—so much,
Is not a staff to trust, but a weak crutch.

CX.

EXPERIENCE sorrows—as the World moves on—
To find POLITENESS little but a name :
To know—with indignation born of shame—
The age of chivalry—to WOMAN—gone !
Youths take the wall when youths with women meet,
And bid them tread the gutter of the street :
Youths keep the hat on—and with women talk !
Nay, puff tobacco round them, where they walk !
Ah ! if it be my privilege to show
The happier usage of the long ago,
And help to raze from Life its foulest stain,
My humble verse will not be writ in vain.

CXI.

INSULTS TO WOMEN are of crimes the worst :
Who strikes a woman is of God accursed :
Flog him ; take manhood out of him : and doom
The coward-miscreant to a living tomb.

CXII.

What is the love of father, sister, brother,
Of husband, wife, son, lover—all combined,
Compared with love the earth-born owes THE MOTHER ?
The first earth duty of Soul, heart, and mind.
A love that lives through life—that never dies ;
A love that elevates and purifies ;
A love that almost worship justifies.

Ah! MOTHER-LOVE! the dearest, sweetest word
Beings below the Angels ever heard!

CXIII.

Almost as sacred is the name of WIFE:
The Eve of Adam, sent to sweeten Life:
Of its hard labour taking double share,
And bearing burdens man would never bear.
Sweet minister, by words, and thoughts, and deeds,
To all his physical and social needs:
Working for him—in Heaven-accorded light;
His help-mate ever! Know ye not such wives
Who to such duties dedicate their lives?

CXIV.

A woman must be pure: and must *seem* pure:
    Light bearing is a blur: light words are wrongs
That sully, at the least: light looks that lure
    Is crime that to the grosser list belongs:
'Tis not enough to *be* pure: they who vex
The heart-pure, stain the white robe of the sex,
And, if not evil, to foul thoughts entice:
They foster, though they may not sanction, Vice.

CXV.

MEN are what women make them: Age and Youth
Bear witness to that grand—Eternal—Truth!
They steer the bark o'er Destiny's dark wave,
And guide us from the cradle to the grave.

CXVI.

Away with women of new-fangled schools—
   God pardon them—who would unsex the sex :
   Of all her natural " Rights" make ghastly wrecks ;
And let none rule who does not show she rules!
Shadow for substance giving—where they bring
A taint more deadly than an adder's sting.

CXVII.

Contrast! Friend, counsellor, companion, wife,
Cherished for Love, in this, and after, life :
Reflective, prudent, wise, and sweetly kind :
A generous heart, a liberal hand and mind :
   Giving a ready help to each who needs:
Though to her " household " first, as wise and just ;
Yielding with grace, and not because she must :
While she, of greater troubles, takes her share,
   She treats the lesser as the garden weeds,
To be removed, and yet with gentle care,
That flowers as well are not uprooted there.
Thus Love endures through all a chequered life,
   In calm, in sunshine, or when tempest-tost :
   The husband found, a lover is not lost,
The sweetheart still remains—a sweetheart wife!

CXVIII.

She waits the husband's home-come, to prepare
The condiments that sweeten humble fare :
Welcome—accorded less by words than looks ;
Precepts—Examples—from the Book of Books

Her Magna Charta and her Bill of Rights,
Are these: God aid her as for these she fights!

CXIX.

Seek a pure " stock," in WEDLOCK: always know
  The father and the mother: are they pure?
  Ill comes of ill—no adage is more sure;
And children's children social taints will show.
  Disease inherited time cannot cure:
From tainted sources, tainted streams *must* flow:
On healthy trees the healthy fruit will grow.

CXX.

Age has its loveliness no less than youth:
For kindness, gentleness, and love, and truth,
Make beauty—beautiful at every stage:
Make beauty—beautiful at any age:
  For-ever beautiful is that sweet face
  In which a tender sympathy we trace:
  A charm that gives it almost sacred grace.
Such beauty counts not years, but laughs at Time;
Such beauty will be always in its prime.

CXXI.

INGRATITUDE! no penalty is thine:
  Thy crime no law can touch: no earth-judge try:
Thy punishment must be by Law Divine!
  Thy sentence be pronounced by God on High!

CXXII.

But GRATITUDE—the Soul's true Wisdom—brings
  The meed of recompense, in many ways:
  A natural law, that all but man obeys,
Is taught to man by all created things:
  The loftiest and the lowest: nothing lives
  That, in return for bounties, nothing gives.
  He who "by owing owes not," pays—and yet
  Is left the richer by a cancelled debt.

CXXIII.

Methinks I hear the Saviour say,
"Where are the nine?" Ah! where are they?
But one returns to praise and pray!
Alas! we search Creation through,
To find of grateful hearts how few:
Alas! the truth is sad as true.
We take the much, the little give:
And for ourselves alone we live.
Lord! Pardon! if the sin be mine:
If I am of the thankless nine:
  If I to Thee no part repay
  Of bounties, given me, day by day,
In boons and blessings that are Thine.

CXXIV.

Strive to PROGRESS: no effort made to rise
  Is Nature outraged, and is God defied.
Progress is proof the living do not die:

The stagnant Soul that never " onward " cries,
    Is one who loiters by the river side,
And waits to cross until the stream runs by.

CXXV.

Whate'er their lot—or what it seems to thee—
All men may rise—if God the Helper be.
    We know that God will find us fit employ:
We know that—very often—social worth
Gives loftier social rank than wealth or birth :
The Patriarchs tilled their fields, their flocks they fed,
Although the armies of the Lord they led :
    And what was David but a shepherd-boy ?

CXXVI.

How many, British-born, of humble birth,
Have risen—to be Lords of Sea and Earth,
Have gained—what birth-boon gave them not—a name :
Made—rightly, proudly, made—by self-wrought fame :
Soil, or coal, delvers, weavers at the loom,
Have had these grand words written on their tomb—
" HERE NATURE'S NOBLE RESTS : " to whom a debt
Is due—Humanity can ne'er forget !

CXXVII.

Take this : a line that does not need a verse :
Nought is so bad, but that it might be worse.

CXXVIII.

If you compare your lot with others' lot :
Remember they have trials you have not :
At best, 'tis dangerous habit to compare
Your ills with those you think have lesser share.
'Tis a far wiser plan—of that be sure—
To think *their* troubles *you* could not endure :
To shrink from those that are to others sent,
Is discipline to mind, and brings content.

CXXIX.

God to the BURTHEN FITS THE BACK : and none
   Have loads so heavy, they can bear no more :
But some will magnify the tasks they shun ;
   Like geese that stoop to pass through a barn door.

CXXX.

When chill winds, fog and sleet, and darkness shroud
   The sun : they keep the sky-lark from the skies :
   They pass : the sky-lark will again arise,
To sing his matin song above the cloud.
To-day may be a day of gloom and sorrow :
Hope ! wait ! all may be bright and glad, to-morrow !

CXXXI.

Let us conceive an Earth-state, always freed
From toil, pain, sorrow, suffering, care, and need :
Yet with no sympathies, no natural ties,
No Earth-love—none that lives but never dies :

May we not safely think that such a state
Infers no coveted or envied fate ?
It is a stagnant pool, no fount supplies.

CXXXII.
A prayer comprising many prayers, indeed !
" God ! give not what we ASK, but what we NEED !"

CXXXIII.
Be careful what you PROMISE CHILDREN : they
Think o'er a promise made : think night and day.
Be more than careful, near them, what you say.
For little ears are long ears, and you may
Plant seed by words : long hidden in the ground,
For good or ill, the fruitage will be found.

CXXXIV.
" Cast bread upon the waters :" after days,
   Or weeks, or years, it shall be found again !
   No good deed done was ever done in vain.
Even in a worldly sense, a good deed " pays."

CXXXV.
YOUNG PILGRIMS ! ere you sleep—before you pray—
Pass in review the doings of the day :
Do nought you cannot ask your God to bless,

But on some duties lay a double stress.
Ask—are there any better that I live?
Ask—those who injured me did I forgive?
Ask—what sad suffering soul have I relieved?
Ask—how shown gratitude for boons received?
Ask—have I said no thoughtless, heedless, word?
Ask—have I told no idle tale I heard?
Ask—has ill-temper ruled, or did I rule?
Ask—have I patience learned in sorrow's school?
Ask—have I caused no creature needless pain?
Ask—when by pleasure lured did I refrain?
Ask—have my bounds of knowledge been enlarged?
Ask—have my duties all been well discharged?
Ask—have I rescued any soul from sin?
Ask—have I any helped the goal to win?
Ask—have I gained, or have I lost a day?
Ask—have I earned by work the right to play?
Ask—have I studied well the lesser graces?
Ask—have I left things in their proper places?
Ask—have I finished all I had begun?
Ask—have I heard my parents say " well done?"
Ask—when with conscience closeted alone—
Ask—Him, to whom all secret thoughts are known—
Ask—that all things—the greater and the less—
You do, and think, and say, your God will bless!
Ask—so that you may hear the Master say,
" Pray—'good and faithful servant'—ask and pray?"
Good angels round you watch and ward will keep,
And a calm Conscience bring refreshing sleep!

CXXXVI.

Of little ones, the Master tells us this:
  " *Their angels* do behold my Father's face
In Heaven:" their home, their hallowed dwelling place:
With love unchanging and eternal bliss,
Their mission, He has told us, is to guide
    The young: and ours to help them in their work,
    Where foes assail, or hidden dangers lurk:
As watchful guardians ever by their side.

CXXXVII.

The young should woo the old: 'tis good and wise:
    Let youth distrust the force of embryo powers:
Nor warning counsels of the old despise.
And age should be indulgent to the young:
Nor use too much that worst of rods—the tongue:
Each vigour brings to each: the hardy breeze
Strengthens mild airs that bless the budding trees:
    The union brings to Earth its fruit and flowers.

CXXXVIII.

Suspicion is a sneaking vice, that takes
    The name of Prudence, and wears Caution's cloak
That sees through spectacles himself he makes
    To suit his scrutiny of other folk.
In evil's chain 'tis of its strongest links;
Does evil, evil speaks, and evil thinks.

CXXXIX.

CANDOUR may be the mate of CAUTION: nay,
The one may help the other, day by day.
It is not needful all we think to say;
But trusty frankness will be frankly met,
And confidence will confidence beget.

CXL.

SPEAK LITTLE, BUT HEAR MUCH, is Wisdom's plan;
God gave two ears, and but one tongue, to man.
This is a truth the wisest man has told
In substance—speech is silver, silence gold.
BE SLOW IN JUDGMENT: merciful in judging:
To rightly judge, nor time nor labour grudging.

CXLI.

A good day's work may end before mid-day,
  And when the work is done, and rightly done,—
You will have earned your pleasure or your play:
  Night cometh, when the work will be for none.

CXLII.

That "GODLINESS and CLEANLINESS are twins,"
  Is truth the old should on the young impress:
Dirt and untidiness are minor sins—
  Perhaps—yet are Home curses, none the less.
The lessons taught by Nature are the best:
The lowest creature will keep pure the nest.

CXLIII.

Revenge! it is the Devil's choicest lure;
   The bait that takes when other temptings fail:
   A dooméd craft that floats without a sail:
A sin, repentance cannot calm or cure.
" Wild Justice," as Revenge the Essayist calls,
   Is oft ferocious parent of Remorse:
Has no ally in Reason: but appals
   By maniac Passion—leading Brutal Force.

CXLIV.

Ask this: " A wounded spirit who can bear?"
Chief of the miseries that mortals share,
   Is SELF-REPROACH: remorse: a living tomb:
   A prospect, and a retrospect, of gloom:
Where can the self-convicted hide it? where?
Remorse without Repentance is but vain,
And barren as the husk without the grain.

CXLV.

Among the greater blessings is CONTENT:
   It brings a world of unalloyed delight;
   And is to mind what beauty is to sight.
   A GRUMBLER is a plague, a household pest:
   Who turns to gloom " the sunshine of the breast."
That brings its own perpetual punishment.

CXLVI.

And study more what you can DO WITHOUT,
But less what you may wish for: when in doubt,
Postpone it—'tis by far the wiser way—
And let the will have act some other day!

CXLVII.

Men's foes are often their best friends: they scare
   The daring, warn the careless: and compel
To caution: dreading a perpetual snare.
   There may be better cause for acting well,
But fear is wholesome—of what foes may say:
Even though they be but pebbles in your way.
" Ever your good name keep—'tis quickly gone :
'Tis gained by many actions—lost by one! "

CXLVIII.

Bear DISAPPOINTMENTS: they are sure to come :
   Think, when you are not getting what you need—
   Or think you need—from perils you are freed.
Perils that loving Mercy keeps you from:
So, meet them, one by one, when they arise,
As tonic medicines of the Great All-wise.

CXLIX.

Shun the unwholesome and unsavoury pleasures,
The length and breadth of which no honour measures.

E

CHANCE GAMES: where gain is robbery or worse.
  Devils in flesh and disembodied devils
  Preside o'er earth-fed and infernal revels :
Helpers' confederate : each brings its curse.

CL.

When SICKNESS comes—as come it will and must—
That is the season for especial trust :
It may be mercy lent—by Angels brought :
  A boon of blessed spirits—sent to give
  A final warning, that we die to live :
Or it may be a call to solemn thought :
A summons back from Death's half-open door,
A glimpse obtained of the celestial shore.

CLI.

A conscious coward is the man who shrinks
  From DEATH : and fears to conquer in the strife :
The cradle and the coffin are but links
  In the weak chain that binds to earth-born life.

CLII.

We live with Angels! they are always near :
  To guard us when we wake and when we sleep :
  Perpetual vigils, night and day, they keep :
Our thoughts they know, and all we say they hear.

CLIII.

Hypocrisy is but an acted lie :
The hypocrite will revel in a stye :
A nasty vice that its own stench betrays :
   That dons a stolen robe, and skulks in state :
   Just as a clown a king may imitate :
Yet 'tis the homage Vice to Virtue pays.

CLIV.

Who dares to say that " Ignorance is Bliss ? "
Such consolation is a Judas kiss !
Who dares to say—and evidence to bring—
" A *little* learning is a dangerous thing ? "
Ay, if the Little seek no larger share,
And Ignorance will vend no sinful ware.

CLV.

Pleasure is not all pleasure : counterpoise
Is Nature's contribution to its joys.
Drawback is written on Life's every page,
Uncertainty the lot of every age.

CLVI.

The breath of life, the anchor of the Soul,
That holds, when tempests rage and billows roll,
Is Hope : no child of Earth is ever born,
No earth-state left so utterly forlorn,

Where Hope is quite shut out: Hope never dies;
Down-beaten, crushed, again will Hope arise!
The sun whose " set " we see, has not left Earth,
   He goes to give to other lands his light:
   He goes and leaves us but awhile with night,
To come back, strong as on his day of birth.

CLVII.

FAITH is but CONFIDENCE in GOD: who gives
Hope, as a beacon light to all that lives:
Hope, to the lowest type of Nature's dearth:
Hope, to the meanest thing that crawls the earth:
Hope, in its garnered harvest to the bee:
Hope, in the promise of the leafless tree:
Hope, as the chiefest boon to human kind:
   Hope, to the Angel host we cannot see:
Hope, nourisher of Soul, of heart, of mind:
   Hope, that is born of Trust—of FAITH IN THEE!

CLVIII.

If the Omnipotent had said to thee,
" Ask what thou wilt: and that my gift shall be,"
What would you say in answer?   Would you crave
Perpetual life—exemption from the grave?
The power that comes with plethora of wealth?
A spirit buoyant with unbroken health?
With men of loftiest rank to read your name?
To hold high place among the heirs of fame?

The courage firm no fear of man alloys?
A keener appetite for sensual joys?
A vigour that no labour tries or tires?
Means to content unlimited desires?
No! No! for this your answering prayer should be—
Give me, Almighty God, more FAITH IN THEE!

CLIX.

Within the Temple slept the child,
    The destined guard of Israel's fame,
When o'er his slumbers, calm and mild,
    The summons of JEHOVAH came.
The call was heard : the child awoke :
    With beating heart, and bended knee,
The after judge and prophet spoke,
    " Speak, Lord, Thy servant heareth Thee."
Oh, when we hear JEHOVAH'S voice
    Stilling the tumults of the soul,
So may we rise, and so rejoice,
    So bend our wills to His control.
His summons calls us even now :
    Oh! may each instant answer be,
" Father, to Thy commands I bow,
    Speak, for Thy servant heareth Thee."

CLX.

And PATIENCE! patient be at work or play :
It keeps a thousand miseries at bay :

And stands a vast amount of wear and tear :
By one sweet rule—to "BEAR AND TO FORBEAR ! "

CLXI.

And never seek a QUARREL : rather shrink
　　From that which must be evil : win or lose :
　　But if it *must* be ; if you cannot choose :
　　Be resolute : be sure that you are right—
And always pray for guidance while you think.
　　Be firm and confident in God-given might.
From Passion what unnumbered evils flow !
Who conquers Passion conquers his worst foe !

CLXII.

A wise man in a passion ! in that hour
Becomes a fool that fools have in their power !

CLXIII.

When wrong, to *own you have been wrong*, is right,
　　Infers no degradation ; the best men
　　Have found themselves in error, now and then.
And nobly, gracefully, retired from fight.
To change opinion, may be but to say
" I am more wise to-day, than yesterday."

CLXIV.

Be RESOLUTE : not OBSTINATE ; the two
　　Are no relations ; though one apes the other :
　　And sometimes claims to be the elder brother :

The one is righteous, holy, just, and true:
The other, deadly nightshade, bitter rue.

CLXV.

Few steal or murder; yet how very few
  From evil wish are scathless : few or none.
But what we will, yet lack the power, to do;
  BE IT FOR GOOD OR ILL GOD COUNTS AS DONE.

CLXVI.

Teachers may not be doers of God's word:
Their tongues may labour, yet no heart be stirred:
Mouth-homage and lip-honour : "gifts" they place
Upon "the Altar :" yet dare ask for Grace.
These are the words the good apostle said—
THE WORKS SHOW FAITH—"faith without works is dead!"
(Dives, in torment, for his brethren prayed:)
He who gives words, but gives no other aid—
  Who says "be warmed and filled"—yet never brings,
  To him who needs them, any of "those things,"
  Takes a poor message from the King of Kings!

CLXVII.

PRAYERS are the wings of love: not learned by rote:
Nor as the cuckoo learns the cuckoo note:
  Prayer may be audible to God alone:
And yet no word be said: Souls breathe in prayer:
Prayer means a prayerful spirit, when or where,
  It matters not—to God it will be known.

CLXVIII.

No matter how you WORSHIP, when or where:
   In the lone glen or in the crowded street:
   (That is a church wherever God you meet:
   Our God is present, where on God we call,
   "The Church *within thy house*," writes holy Paul:)
Good spirits and good angels wait you there.
If you gain Heaven, will guarding angels say
"Go back, and find to Heaven a better way?"
They are not messengers of God who teach
That there are souls His voice can never reach:
The shrivelled, cruel, cold, and selfish creed,
That but ONE narrow road to Heaven *can* lead!

CLXIX.

Away with those who tell us God is gloom,
   Who make a bugbear of RELIGION, try
   To humble God, as utterer of a lie,—
And show us Mercy as pernicious doom.
Religion is to comfort and console:
   To mind and heart what sunshine is to flowers,
   Cheering and giving strength, as do spring showers.
Far more than that—it nourishes the Soul!
   Those who but tell us of an angry God—
   Who hides His Staff and only shows His Rod,
   A God, but not of Love—a God to dread—
   Vilely interpret all He did and said.
Avoid them : give such teachers natural ban :
They are the worst and deadliest foes of man.

CLXX.

Let SCIENCE sneer at Faith ; and REASON frown ;
And prove there are no Souls to argue down :
Admit a God—though much too old to learn,
Or they might teach Him lessons, in their turn.
Can Science gauge the influence that draws
   The needle to the magnet ?   Can it see
The perfume of the rose ?   Or measure laws
   By which the flower gives honey to the bee ?
Can Reason see—and not with scornful smiles—
Words, in a second, run a thousand miles ?
Can Reason hear what fellow mortals say
In whispers, breathed a hundred miles away ?

CLXXI.

They limit the Omnipotent to acts
   That Science calls " the possible," and thus,
Binding the Infinite to rules and facts,
   Explain " the fable of the Soul " to us.
Ten thousand thousand things, exist we know,
   By SCIENCE tested, and by REASON tried,
With no conclusive issue, save to show
   How much we need a better LIGHT AND GUIDE.
In tortuous paths, with prompters blind, we trust
   ONE GUIDE—to lead us forth and set us free !
Give us, Lord God ! all merciful and just !
   The FAITH that is but CONFIDENCE IN THEE !

CLXXII.

Such shallow dippers into Nature's laws,
     Try Nature's powers by five unerring tests—
     The Soul's directing and controlling guests!
Can they the oak within the acorn see?
Or in the egg, the feathers, beak, and claws?
Yet one will be the eagle : one the tree.

CLXXIII.

The whale and shark were oysters once, no doubt :
     And elephants were magnified from—mice :
Eagles were beetles, ere their plumes came out :
     And trees were fungi—when the sun was ice !
It took some time to bring these things about :
To make of nothings somethings : " Countless Ages ! "
The work being done—per Chance—at several stages.

CLXXIV.

Science but needs the nut to find the kernel,
     And only wants the seed to plant the seed.
But though it can't admit a God Eternal,
     Eternal MATTER is a simple creed.
Aided by Senses five—unerring tests !
     That never can be more, and never less,
     Assisted by the great Logician—GUESS,
They close the lips of all believing pests !

CLXXV.

Remember, TEMPERANCE is like Samson's hair :
The source of Power, Philistia did not dare,
Till Sin consigned him to the Siren's lair.

CLXXVI.

Men purchase pleasures only fiends will sell,
And barter peace and health for joys of Hell!

CLXXVII.

What is the Drunkard's life ?   A life of pain,
　　Of sin, of sorrow, self-reproach, and shame,
Of home-affliction : evil wants, that drain
The home-resources : leave a filthy stain
　　On all its sacred ties : dishonoured name !
Friends, estimate the loss, and count the gain !
Shun, as a plague, THE DRINK : a glimpse of light—
It may be—heralding a dismal night.

CLXXVIII.

Ask judges, jailers, coroners,—ask all
　　Who have to do with wrong, and sin, and crime :
　　What most envelops man in filth and slime ?
Whence come the peril-crimes that most appall ?
Ask what philanthropists, what doctors, think ?
　　Where foul diseases are a frightful host ?
　　Where Satan, Sin, and Death, will triumph most ?
All, all, will give one answer—" Drink ! drink ! drink !"

CLXXIX.

Think! oh think!   Oh! women, do not drink!
  Women who are, or may be, home-blest wives,
O'er the dark gulf you stand—upon the brink,
  May have, and give your children, blighted lives:
For be ye sure the children share the curse
Of woe, transmitted by the mother-nurse.
  Can *you* have sober husbands if *you* drink?
Can you have healthful children if you bear
Children to Drunkards, and *you* take *your* share?
Children who trace to you the sin and shame
That from a sinful, shameful, mother came;
Children who live to curse you in your grave
For the hereditary curse you gave?

CLXXX.

You who have driven the Drink-fiend from your houses,
  Hold up your good right hands!

You who abjure false pleasures, foul carouses,
  With stern resolve to bear the curse no more:
  Hold up your good right hands!

  You of our TEMPERANCE BANDS,
Who give the drinking den your heaviest ban,
  And turn, with loathing pity, from the door
Of him who prospers by corrupting man,
  The young, the old, the wealthy, and the poor:

  HOLD UP YOUR GOOD RIGHT HANDS!

CLXXXI.

God bless the conquering BANDS OF HOPE!
　　　God bless
The young first fruits of Righteousness!
　　　God bless
The men and women good, who lead them!
　　　God bless
　All soldiers of the glorious bands!
　　　God bless
　The conquering troop of many lands!
Those who love God will pray "God speed" them!

CLXXXII.

We are BANDS OF HOPE!   Come, hear our song:
　And join us in the song we raise:
　A song of mingled love and praise:
While gleefully we march along:
In faith, in health, in vigour, strong.
We are BANDS OF HOPE—young girls and boys!
Who bid you share their simple joys.
We drink pure water from the spring:
　We touch no vile accurséd drink;
　And, children though we are, we think.
Good Angels hear the song we sing.
Armed for the certain war of life,
We dread no danger in the strife:
No foes with whom we cannot cope—
We—soldiers in the BANDS OF HOPE.
We are the Future! we who thus

Are strengthened as our lives begin,
    Avoiding all the ways of sin:
Good men and women helping us.
Our Pastors teach the holy plan—
That love of God is love of man.
We BANDS OF HOPE, we march along,
While Angels hear and join our song!

CLXXXIII.

But above all—in God have Faith and Trust!
Strive to be numbered with the " Perfect Just."
In all you say or do, ask help from God!
So shall you bear His staff, and 'scape His rod.

CLXXXIV.

Such lessons Age and Wisdom teach the young
To guide, and rule, the heart, the mind, the tongue.
    But not to youth alone—at any age
    Such maxims govern life : at every stage!
    Such maxims make the humblest man a sage!

CLXXXV.

Lessons they are, that Age should teach to Youth:
Lessons of Old Experience, Wisdom, Truth:
    Lessons of gathered knowledge, garnered thought!
    By wise men and by Holy Prophets taught!
    The counsels and the warnings of all Time!

GOD GIVE A BLESSING TO MY HUMBLE RHYME!

FAREWELL!

Through mists that hide me from my God, I see
A shapeless form : Death comes, and beckons me :
I scent the odours of the Spirit land :
   And, with commingled joy and terror, hear
The far-off whispers of a white-robed band :—
   Nearer they come—yet nearer—yet more near :
Is it rehearsal of a " Welcome " song
That will be in my heart and ear, ere long?
Do these bright spirits wait till Death may give
The Soul its franchise—and I die to live?

Does fancy send the breeze from yon green mountain?
   (I am not dreaming when it cools my brow.)
Are they the sparkles of an actual fountain
   That gladden and refresh my spirit now
How beautiful the burst of holy light!
How beautiful the day that has no night!
Open! ye everlasting gates! I pray—
Waiting, but yearning—for that perfect day!

Hark! to these Alleluias! " hail! all hail!"
Shall *they* be echoed by a sob and wail?
Friends, " gone before," these are your happy voices :
The old, familiar, sounds: my soul rejoices!

Ah! through the mist, the great white throne I see :
And now a Saint in glory beckons me.
Is Death a foe to dread? the Death who giveth
Life—the unburthened Life that ever liveth!

Who shrinks from Death? Come when he will or may,
The night he brings will bring the risen day:
His call—his touch—we neither seek nor shun:
His life is ended when his work is done.
Our spear and shield no cloud of Death can dim:
He triumphs not o'er us,—we conquer him!

How long, O Lord, how long, ere I shall see
     The myriad glories of a holier sphere?
     And worship in Thy presence?—not as here
In chains that keep the shackled Soul from Thee!

     My God! let that Eternal Home be near!

Master! I bring to Thee a Soul opprest:
"Weary and heavy laden:" seeking rest:
Strengthen my Faith; that, with my latest breath,
I greet Thy messenger of Mercy—DEATH!

FINIS.

www.ingramcontent.com/pod-product-compliance
Lightning Source LLC
Chambersburg PA
CBHW030010030726
47499CB00008B/2988